Koko & Friends

The Long Shots

Clara Denise West, Ph.D.

Copyright © 2022 by Clara Denise West

All rights reserved under International and Pan-American Copyright Conventions. No part of this book may be reproduced or utilized in any form or by any means, electronic or mechanical, including photocopying, recording or by any information storage and retrieval system, without permission in writing from the Publisher.

Koko and Friends Products
Brooklyn, New York

E-mail: claradenisewest39@gmail.com
www.kokoandfriends.com

The names, characters, and the Koko and Friends logo are all trademarks of Clara Denise West. Applications for registration of the aforementioned character names and the Koko and Friends logo have been filed with the U. S. Patent and Trademarks Office.

International Standard Book Number: 978-1-892313-02-7
Library of Congress Number: 2022903344
Printed in the United States of America

Acknowledgements

My heartfelt appreciation is extended to my children – Daniel and Charla. Thanks for the endless hours you spent reviewing and editing this book.

To my Bella Bee, the sweetest granddaughter in the world, you are the candles on my cake.

To my daughter-in-love, Dwayna, thank you for doing whatever was needed to make this book possible. Love you, my second daughter.

I would like to extend a special "Thank You" to my SCORE mentors, Jack Cohn and Maurice Bretzfield. Accept my heartfelt gratitude for your advice, guidance, and feedback.

Many thanks go out to Stephania Darby, Cynthia Scales, Susan Leister, Susan Boger, Deb Goemans, Arlette Fletcher, and every kindred spirit at the New York Women in Film and Television (NYWIFT) New Works Lab for your critiques and suggestions.

This book is dedicated to the memory of my parents, John and Clara West.

To my Best Friend, Thank You.

Foreword

I support the Golden Rule strategy for modeling behavior and the value-based decision process inherent in the *Koko and Friends* storylines. Through *Koko and Friends* products, children can learn that there is nothing funny about name-calling, bullying, or ridiculing other children who look, behave, or learn in a way that is different from them. The characters, like children, occasionally make bad decisions, yet they are taught to learn from their mistakes.

Children are getting multiple, and sometimes unhealthy, messages from media and society. I believe that the *Koko and Friends Project* can positively impact young people. Children can learn important social and interdependence skills that will help them throughout their life. It takes courage and a strong sense of integrity to live according to the Golden Rule when dealing with competitive group dynamics. Parents, caregivers, and educators can use the characters or situations in the books as a perfect opportunity to talk to children about topics like self-discipline, respect, and goal setting.

Dr. Elliot Aronson
Professor Emeritus, University of California in Santa Cruz
Distinguished Author and Researcher

Contents

PART 1: THE BACKGROUND STORY 1

   Chapter 1: The Day of The Fog 3

   Chapter 2: Welcome to the Family!........................ 15

   Chapter 3: Let's Play Ball! 21

   Chapter 4: And the Journey Begins........................ 29

   Chapter 5: Ants With an Attitude! 33

   Chapter 6: Unkind Ladybugs 39

   Chapter 7: The Webs They Weave 47

   Chapter 8: Pelted! 55

   Chapter 9: All That Glitters 61

   Chapter 10: Hurt, but Not Broken! 67

   Chapter 11: The Experiment 75

   Chapter 12: Think About It! 79

   Chapter 13: Meet the Girls 85

   Chapter 14: Practice is Work! 91

PART 2: THE NEIGHBORHOOD FRENEMIES 99

   Chapter 15: Friends. Or. Not?................................ 101

   Chapter 16: It's Decision Time! 107

   Chapter 17: Party or Part!...................................... 111

   Chapter 18: Oops!... 117

Chapter 19: I'm Back! 125

Chapter 20: My Bad! 129

Chapter 21: Friendship Kinship 135

Chapter 22: Principles and Integrity 141

Chapter 23: Pay the Piper! 145

NOTE TO PARENTS **149**

PART 1
THE BACKGROUND STORY

Chapter 1
The Day of The Fog

In a small, neatly-kept red-brick bungalow lives an ordinary family of four humans. Their modestly furnished house has three bedrooms, two baths, a family room, a sunroom, a kitchen, and a basement laundry room.

Unknown to the humans who live upstairs, the basement laundry room is the heart of the house bugs' world. Spiders, beetles, earwigs, ants, centipedes, termites, roaches, and a melting pot of other bugs live under the water heater, dryer, window sills, ceiling beams, storage cabinets–and anywhere else they can call "home". Bugs of every species and walk-of-life come here seeking fun, fame, and fortune. Even young bug-couples bring their unhatched eggs here to build their nests and raise their families.

Under the water heater lives a family of eleven undefeated basketball-playing sisters. They were just voted All-Stars among the basement teams. The ten older sisters are married to basketball players. They are eagerly looking forward to the day when their eggs hatch and they become parents to the next generation of All-Stars.

The sisters' father, Grandpa Jack, is also their coach. He hopes that his daughters will one day compete against teams beyond the basement. He knows they can easily become All-Star champions of the whole bungalow.

Then came the day of The Fog. The basement they knew before The Fog no longer exists. Their once thriving bug world was completely destroyed.

Grandpa Jack sighs and rocks back and forth in his favorite chair as he watches over the ten precious 'soon-to-hatch' eggs. He begins to daydream. He recalls the times when his own beautiful daughters hatched. His smile fades when he remembers the sad day that started so full of fun, hope, and laughter. His daughters, the mothers of these eggs, were celebrating their future arrivals. What happened that day came without warning.

One of the humans who lives upstairs comes into the basement and changes their lives forever. The human walks to the center of the laundry room and places a crystal ball on the floor. He presses a button on top of it, rushes up the stairs, and closes the door.

The ball begins to spin and whistle. Several bugs dare to come out from their hiding places to get a closer look of the spinning, whistling object. One of the ants slowly creeps close enough to the ball to touch it.

"Wow. I wonder what it is?" asks the ant thoughtfully.

An earwig joins him. He thumps it and replies, "I have no idea. I've never seen anything like this before."

The ball spins faster and whistles louder. A crowd quickly gathers.

A centipede steps out from the crowd and knocks on the sphere. He says, "Sounds like it's full of some type of liquid." He knocks on it again and continues, "Hmmp, I don't know what it is, but I don't like the way it sounds. It's too scary for me. I'm out of here."

As the centipede scurries off, a pillbug grunts, "Ahh, leave already! You're scared of everything."

The crystal ball spins faster and faster. It whistles louder and louder. Suddenly, the button on top of the ball begins to make a clicking sound as if it's snapping its fingers.

"What kind of music is that?" asks one of the beetles.

The ant replies, "It could be some kind of new pop tune."

Another small group of bugs joins them as they form a circle around the mysterious spinning, whistling object.

All of a sudden, the ball begins to rock back and forth as it releases a white, sweet-smelling fog. One of the water bugs takes a deep breath and says, "Mmm, that smells so good. It reminds me of—"

An ant in the group takes a deep breath and coughs, "UCK. IT'S ... IT'S POISON!'

"POISON?" asks one of the earwigs. "DID YOU SAY POISON?"

The ant grabs his throat, falls to the floor, and passes out.

The earwig turns to the other bugs and yells, "DON'T COME ANY CLOSER... RUN!" The earwig tries to escape, but he is quickly overtaken by The Fog.

The group of bugs that surround the ball run as fast as they can to find a safe place. The slower moving water bugs cry out, "WE'RE... DYING...(COUGH)... RUNNN!"

Many of the bugs try to run to their homes for cover only to find The Fog has beat them there. Most are quickly overtaken.

A termite leaves her nest in the wall to see what's happening. When she sees The Fog, she scurries across the floor and yells, "THE FOG...IT'S COMING. RUN..." Several bugs that are far away from the ball hear the warning and run towards the washer seeking cover.

Flies in the garbage barrel are awakened by screams and cries from the other bugs. Annoyed because their sleep is disturbed, they leave their nests to find the source of the noise. The Fog has expanded high enough into the air that the flies fly straight into it. They instantly fall to the floor.

Several bugs run under the washer where a community baby shower is taking place. They scream, "POISON... POISON... THE FOG IS COMING.... RUN..."

Grandpa Jack's eleven daughters are attending the baby shower when they hear the warning. They look out only to see the thick white fog coming towards them. The oldest sister screams, "Oh, no! Our eggs. We've got to save our eggs!"

The oldest sister turns to her younger sisters and says, "Grab as many eggs as you can carry, hold your breath, and run as fast as you can to the water heater. It's sealed off from the rest of the laundry room!"

The older ten sisters make it to the water heater and push their eggs inside the pilot door. Lovelady, their much smaller younger sister, struggles to run as she stumbles under the weight of the eggs. The oldest sister turns around and runs back to help her. She covers her little sister's nose and mouth with her wings and pushes her to the water heater.

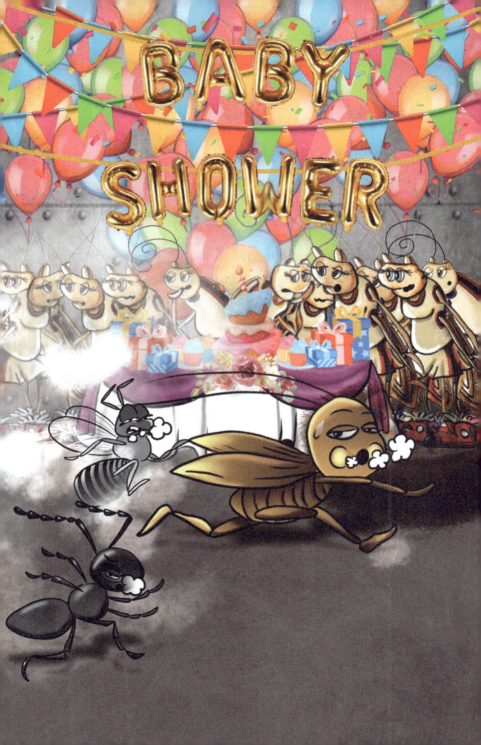

Once they make it through the water heater door, the oldest sister pushes Lovelady and the eggs she's carrying into the hallway. She runs back to the washer to gather more eggs.

Grandpa Jack and the husbands of the ten older sisters are building nursery furniture in the breezeway of the water heater when they hear the uproar. They rush to the hallway to find Lovelady on her knees gasping for air. She crumbles at Grandpa Jack's feet, points to the door, and cries, "PAPA... THE FOG... THEY NEED HELP!"

The husbands jump to their feet and prepare to help their wives save their eggs. Grandpa Jack tries to join them. Lovelady pleads, "PAPA, NO!"

The husband of the oldest sister looks at Grandpa Jack and agrees, "Stay here. We need to hand the eggs to you when we get to the door so we can go back and gather more eggs." Grandpa Jack nods his head.

The husbands run between the washer and water heater several times before The Fog overtakes them. After inhaling the poison, nine older sisters and all ten husbands die.

The oldest sister crawls back to the water heater and makes her way through the pilot door. She falls to the floor as she struggles to breathe. Lovelady and Grandpa Jack run to her side. The oldest sister weakly grips Grandpa Jack's hand and wheezes, "I'm... not... going... to... make... it. (COUGH)... Promise me... our eggs... raise them... love them—"

Lovelady gently weeps, "No, you're going to be ok!"

The oldest sister looks desperately at Grandpa Jack and struggles to say, "Papa... promise... me..."

Grandpa Jack silently weeps, "You know I will!"

She turns to Lovelady and searches her face. She squeezes her youngest sister's hand as she whispers, "Promise..."

Lovelady nods her head and softly cries, "I promise."

The oldest sister gasps a sigh of relief as a single tear rolls slowly down her cheek. She exhales and she's gone.

Lovelady crumbles on top of her sister's chest and cries, "No... Don't go..." Grandpa Jack lifts Lovelady to her feet as they weep for his daughters.

Out of the thousand eggs his daughters laid, only ten survived The Fog—one from each daughter. Although Grandpa Jack and Lovelady are heartbroken about their losses, they are excited about the ten eggs and what the future holds.

In that moment they notice how the eggs glow and look so rich when the light from the water heater pilot hits them. Lovelady says, "These little eggs are now orphans. I've always been the baby of the family and everyone has taken care of me. I don't know anything about being an aunt or mother. What if I don't know what to do?"

Grandpa Jack takes off his spectacles and wipes tears from his eyes. Lovelady moves closer to him and gives him a hug.

"These eggs are all we have left of my daughters," says Grandpa Jack. "Please don't cry, Papa. I miss them, too," whispers Lovelady. She suddenly realizes how heartbroken he is. He lost ten of his eleven daughters to The Fog.

"I want to move the girl eggs to my room. I have more than enough space," says Lovelady as she kneels down to move one of the eggs closer to the pilot light. The little bug inside stretches and kicks back against her hand. "Wow," she laughs. "That was a hard kick. This one is really a fighter."

She adds thoughtfully, "You know, Papa, it's a long shot they survived The Fog. Even as eggs, they've proven to be survivors. Who knows what amazing things they'll accomplish after they hatch. We'll have to teach them not only how to survive, but how to thrive."

Grandpa Jack smiles to himself, puts his spectacles back on, and speaks under his breath, "Hmm.... The Long Shots... That's the perfect team name for them... The Long Shots."

Grandpa Jack checks on the eggs one final time before he turns off the light and goes to bed for the night.

Chapter 2
Welcome to the Family!

It's been over three months since the day of The Fog. The eggs are growing longer each day. Lovelady even thinks she hears yawning and giggling sounds coming from the eggs when she turns them over to make sure they keep warm. It's as if they're playing games with her while still in their shells.

A week later, Grandpa Jack and Lovelady notice the eggs are longer but not moving as much as they were earlier. Grandpa Jack remarks, "It looks like they'll hatch soon. We'll need to watch them closer now."

"Maybe it's time to move the girl eggs to my bedroom and I'll stay there with them until they hatch. Besides, they've gotten so long that they need more room to grow before they hatch," adds Lovelady.

Her bedroom is large and 'girlie' with pink and purple decorations. It was once the bedroom she shared with three of her ten sisters. There are girl power posters and basketball ribbons hanging on the walls. On the dressers are plaques, medals, and trophies she and her sisters won.

Lovelady and Grandpa Jack move the girl eggs safely to her bedroom. When all the girls eggs are moved, they place the boy eggs closer to the pilot light to make sure they have enough room to stretch. Lovelady then returns to her bedroom to care for the girl eggs.

Grandpa Jack yawns, "I'm tired." He picks up his jTab, reclines in his favorite chair, and begins reading the newsfeed. Soon, the silence of the room and the hum of the gas pilot light in the background send him to sleep.

Grandpa Jack jerks himself awake when he hears increasingly loud thuds and thumps from the five boy eggs as they bask under the water heater pilot light. He gets up and walks over to the eggs to check on them. His antennas twitch as he senses odd movements from the eggs. He looks over his spectacles when he hears—THUD. THUD. THUD. The thuds grow louder and more often.

One of the eggs begins to shake furiously. Grandpa Jack hears a loud popping sound and sees a crack appear near the bottom of the egg. A small foot struggles to push its way through the growing crack. A second foot makes its way out of the shell.

Then, a set of little legs protrude from the egg. A bug wearing a tan, black, and red basketball uniform with 'KOKO #1' stamped on the front of his jersey pops out. Although the shell still covers Koko's head, he jumps to his feet and runs back and forth around the room until the top of the shell hits a wall. The shell crumbles and falls to the floor. Koko stands up and rubs his head. He quickly shakes the remaining pieces of shell off, stretches, grunts, and wipes his eyes as he looks around.

Meanwhile, a second egg cartwheels in circles across the floor and smashes against a wall. Its shell shatters. PREACHER #3 is stamped on his uniform. Preacher hits the floor landing soundly on his bottom. He stands up, stretches, lifts up his eyeglasses, squints, and puts his glasses back on. Preacher shrugs as he slowly looks around the room.

The third egg begins to wobble across the floor before it hits a wall. Suddenly, LUCKY #5, squeezes through a crack in the side of his shell. He's stuck. He struggles but he can't free himself. He takes a sudden quick breath in and lets out an explosive ACHOO!! The force of Lucky's sneeze is so strong that his entire shell pops off in one piece. Startled, Koko and Preacher jump to their feet and look at Lucky with mistrust.

The loud sound of Lucky's sneeze awakens the bug in the fourth egg. The top of his shell cracks and pops off completely. His basketball uniform is stamped with the name STRINGBEAN #7. The tall, big bug sticks his head out of the shell pieces that cling to his neck as he searches for the source of the sneeze. Stringbean shakes off the remains of his shell as he stands to his feet and rubs his eyes.

The fifth egg does not budge. Koko, Preacher, Lucky, and Stringbean surround the egg as they wait for it to hatch. When nothing happens, they move closer to the egg only to hear snoring sounds coming from inside.

At first, Koko gently knocks on the shell and tries to wake up the snoring bug. The egg does not move. Koko and Preacher knock harder and harder. The snoring continues. Lucky and Stringbean join Koko and Preacher as they knock on the egg.

Finally, the shell shatters. TRIPLE POINT #9 flops out of the shell onto the floor. He wakes up and frowns at the other bugs. He stands up, yawns, stretches, and dusts himself off. He looks at his arms and legs to see if the floor-flop caused him any injuries. Triple Point looks at his cousins and asks, "Hey, what gives? I need my sleep."

Grandpa Jack thoroughly inspects each of them. He reads the names on each of their uniforms. "Koko... Preacher... Lucky... Stringbean... Triple Point," he says.

Koko looks at Grandpa Jack and asks, "Wh...Wh...Where am I? Who are you?"

Grandpa Jack answers, "This is your home. I'm your grandfather, Grandpa Jack. Welcome to the world."

Preacher asks, "Who am I?" He points at his cousins and asks, "Who are they?"

"You boys are cousins and your destiny is to play basketball. You hatched in uniforms with your names on your jerseys," replies Grandpa Jack. The confused young bugs look at their uniforms and each other.

"Oh, okay," says Koko.

Grandpa Jack smiles, walks to his chair, and sits down. He lifts his hand and signals the boys to sit in a semi-circle on the floor in front of him. Grandpa Jack declares, "Koko was the first to hatch, so he's your team captain." He looks at Koko and says, "You have a big job ahead of you. Your cousins will look to you for leadership and direction. You'll always have to think about what's best for the team."

Koko replies, "Sweet."

Grandpa Jack stands up and walks to the area where the bugs hatched. He picks up a basketball. "This is a basketball," he says. "Every young basketball player's dream is to become an All-Star." Grandpa Jack bounces the ball and says, "C'mon, boys! Let's go to the gym." The bright-eyed boys gleefully follow him.

Chapter 3
Let's Play Ball!

Grandpa Jack tells the boys, "This is our gym." He opens the door and turns on the lights. The boys follow him in and look around.

The gym, now brightly lit, exposes freshly painted gray and red walls with blue and black trimmings. It is spacious with well-worn, pull-down wooden bleachers. The hardwood floor is perfectly polished.

Grandpa Jack walks to the center of the rectangular room and says, "This is a basketball court."

Koko asks, "What do those lines on the floor mean?"

Grandpa Jack replies, "Hold on, I'm going to get to that in a minute." He turns and points, "At each end of the court, there's a hoop and net called a basket. As basketball players your goal is to shoot this ball through your basket."

Grandpa Jack easily shoots the ball through the basket nearest him.

Koko catches it and bounces it back to him. "Cool." says Koko.

Triple Point asks, "When can I shoot the ball?"

Grandpa Jack replies, "Just hold on a minute. You'll have plenty of time to shoot balls." He turns back to the group. "The game is played between two teams. Each team has five players on the court at a time."

Grandpa Jack walks to the center of the court. The boys follow him. Grandpa Jack points to the line. "This is the mid-court line. It divides the court into halves."

Grandpa Jack dribbles the ball towards the basket. "You can only move the ball down the court towards your basket by either dribbling it or passing it with your hands." He bounces the ball and says, "This is how it's done."

Grandpa Jack dribbles the ball and passes it to Koko.

Koko dribbles and passes the ball to Triple Point. The ball goes from Triple Point to Lucky.

Lucky passes the ball to Stringbean.

Stringbean leaps into the air and easily makes a jump shot.

Koko catches the ball, dribbles it twice, then shoots it through the hoop. He squeals, "Ohhh! I get it! This is fun! I could do this all day!"

The boys take turns dribbling, passing, and shooting the ball.

Stringbean exclaims, "Wow! We've made every basket. We're good! This HAS TO BE our destiny!"

Triple Point turns to Grandpa Jack and asks, "But, how'll we know when we win?"

"The team with the most points at the end of the game wins," explains Grandpa Jack.

Koko asks, "Points? How do you get points?"

Grandpa Jack walks across the court. He says, "If you make a basket anywhere in this area, you score two points." He leads them to the three-point arc on the court and bounces the ball to Triple Point. "If you make a basket behind this curve, you score three points," adds Grandpa Jack.

Triple Point easily shoots a three-point shot. His cousins watch in amazement. Koko catches the ball.

Preacher says, "Wow, that was incredible! How'd you do that?" Triple Point jokes, "Awe. All skill."

Stringbean snickers, "Skill?... You mean you got lucky!"

Lucky turns to the boys and asks, "Hey? Did someone call my name?" His cousins chuckle.

Grandpa Jack adds, "And, a free throw is worth one point."

Lucky asks, "What's a free throw?"

Grandpa Jack replies, "It's a shot that a player gets when a player on the other team has a foul called against him."

The boys look puzzled. Koko asks, "What's a foul?"

Grandpa Jack inhales deeply before replying, "That's not an easy question to answer. You'll understand everything you need to know as you learn the basics of the game. As your coach, my job is to show you how to avoid making fouls."

Koko brags, "We made every basket. I'm sure we won't make any fouls." Grandpa Jack shakes his head and chuckles, "You boys have so much to learn. Right now, just get use to the feel of the ball and the court."

Grandpa Jack walks over to the coach's table.

Koko dribbles the ball and passes it to Lucky. Each of the boys take turns dribbling, passing, and shooting the ball. None of the boys miss any of the baskets they attempt. In fact, Triple Point makes five three-point shots in a row.

Grandpa Jack blows his whistle signaling the boys to stop playing and meet him courtside.

"Koko, as team captain, you'll have to know the rules as well as the strengths and weaknesses of your teammates.

"You'll have to make sure your team is prepared and ready to play other teams," says Grandpa Jack.

Koko asks, "Where do the other teams come from?"

Grandpa Jack replies, "They can come from almost anywhere."

Koko asserts, "As team captain, I say we go and find other teams to play!"

Stringbean cries, "Yeah."

Grandpa Jack warns them, "Slow your roll, boys! You just hatched a few minutes ago. You don't know how to play basketball yet. You haven't even practiced as a team."

Koko responds, "I thought you said basketball is our destiny. What else do we need to know?"

Triple Point adds, "Besides, we haven't missed a basket."

Koko asks, "How'll we ever become All-Stars if we don't play other teams?"

Grandpa Jack tries to reason with the boys, "Becoming All-Star players... that's a HUGE accomplishment that doesn't happen in a few minutes. It takes time and a whole lot of hard work."

"Don't you want us to become All-Stars?" pouts Koko.

Grandpa Jack replies, "Of course I do... But I see there are some lessons you boys will have to learn the hard way," as they walk towards the gym exit.

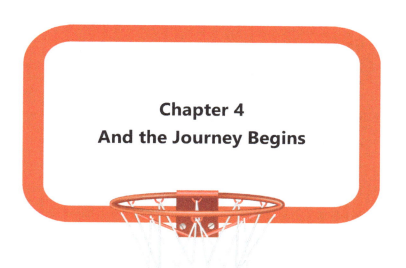

Chapter 4
And the Journey Begins

Grandpa Jack escorts Koko and his cousins to the edge of the water heater. He gives them final words of advice and warnings, "The world beyond this water heater can be as frightening as it is beautiful. Always stay together and look out for each other."

"Yes, sir." replies the boys,

Grandpa Jack warns them again, "Remember—stay together! You'll find strength and safety if you stay together... If you need to warn each other about danger, scream "AIR BALL." That means RUN and don't stop RUNNING until you get to a safe place... Do I make myself clear?"

The boys reply, "Yes, sir!"

Grandpa Jack adds, "Be kind to everyone you meet and always treat them the way you want them to treat you. Our family motto is, 'Do What's Right: If you start right and stay right, you'll end right!'"

"Bye, Grandpa Jack," the boys say in a chorus. Koko adds, "We'll be back as soon as we play some other teams!"

Once they step beyond the water heater, they see the basement is little more than a drab, open laundry room. It's filled with baskets of clothes waiting to be washed or put away. Three shelves are attached to the back wall. A big garbage barrel stands next to two cardboard storage boxes. The washer and dryer are near the shelves. Off in the corner stands the gas water heater, which is where they live.

On the other side of the basement are stairs that lead to the place where the humans live.

As the boys crawl up the stairs, they discuss which way to go.

Koko says, "We've got to find some teams to play. C'mon guys, let's split up so we can cover more space!"

Stunned, Preacher replies, "Koko, did you hear anything Grandpa Jack said? He told us to stay together. You want to break that rule already?"

Koko tries to explain, "Grandpa Jack said if any of us get in trouble just yell 'AIR BALL'—"

Stringbean warns Koko saying, "Yelling won't help if we're so far apart we can't hear or help each other!!!"

Koko says, "But, what if we—"

"NO, Koko!" declares Triple Point, "We're staying together."

Koko grumbles, "You guys are no fun. Let's go!"

Koko and his cousins continue climbing up the dimly lit stairway that leads to the land of the humans. They finally reach the top of the stairs and see the brown door that opens to the kitchen.

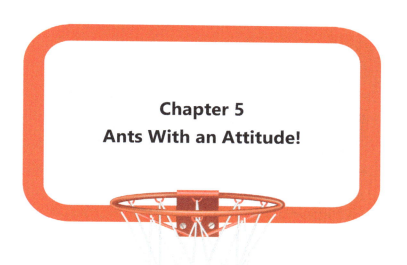

Chapter 5
Ants With an Attitude!

Koko and his cousins enter the kitchen only to discover the brown basement door is white on the other side. Their mouths drop open as they stare in amazement at the beautiful room. The brightly-lit kitchen looks nothing like the dreary basement they just left.

The sun shines through the windows and lights up the whole room. The walls are sky-blue and the blue-gray tiled floor is freshly waxed. Even the musty odor of the basement is replaced with the sweet smells of fresh-baked bread and homemade cookies.

"Wow," says Koko. "This place is full of light. Everything here is so beautiful!"

"Yeah! And, it smells good, too. I'm not sure, but I think I'm hungry," remarks Stringbean.

"We didn't come here to eat. We came here to find another team to play!" replies Preacher.

They look around and see ants all over the place. Two stink ants guard the entrance. A colony of worker ants carry sugar cubes in a straight line across the floor. A richly adorned queen ant is lying under a tent four fire ants fan her. All the ants work to the beat of Arabian music playing in the background.

Koko ponders aloud, "Hmm, I wonder if they'll play with us?"

Triple Point replies, "Just ask them and see."

Stringbean looks at the busy ants and agrees, "Yeah. They might. Ask them."

The boys approach the working ants. Koko smiles at one of them. The ant nods slightly but does not speak to him.

Koko walks up to the ant and politely asks him, "Excuse me... Hi,... Would you guys like to play basketball with us?"

The ant looks at Koko in disbelief and snaps, "You see us carrying these huge sugar cubes on our backs and you have the nerve to ask us if we want to play basketball? WE'RE ANTS. We have too much work to do to play with you!"

A second ant stops walking and angrily says, "Yeah. We have to put away food for our queen."

Preacher curiously asks, "Do you have to work all the time?"

Lucky smiles and says, "Yeah. Can't you take a little break and play basketball with us?"

A third ant walks up to the group and yells, "NO CAN DO! Only lazy bugs have time to play basketball!"

Koko smiles and responds, "You think that maybe if we help you carry some of those sugar cubes to wherever you have to take them, you can make time to play basketball with us?"

The first ant frowns at Koko and snarls, "Did we ask you to help us? Do we look like we need help from lazy bugs like you?"

Triple Point looks at the Queen texting on her phone, nibbling on a sugar cookie, and relaxing under a tent while four fire ants fan her with huge dried palm leaves. Confused, he blurts, "I don't get it. You have to gather food for your Queen while she's playing on her phone and eating cookies? Why can't she get up and get her own food? Are her legs broken or something? You call us lazy bugs, but your Queen looks like the lazy bug to me."

The music stops and silence falls over the room like a heavy blanket. The Queen drops her phone from her hand. The four fire ants drop their fans. All the other ants stop everything they're doing as they look at each other in shock. They all turn and stare angrily at Koko and his cousins.

The army ants march forward in a circle and surround them.

Koko mumbles, "Uh, Oh!"

The first ant gets in Triple Point's face and snaps, "Whoa! Time out, dude! Did you just call our Queen lazy?"

The second ant asks, "Did you dare diss our Queen?"

A row of FIRE ANTS gets into attack position.

Triple Point boldly declares, "Your lazy Queen dissed herself!"

A group of stink ants moves closer to the boys and begins to rub their legs together as they quietly release a foul-smelling gas from their bottoms. Koko and his cousins look at the ants, back away, and cover their noses.

Stringbean says, "Phew! Something stinks!"

The third ant smiles meanly and snaps, "It's our secret attack alarm!"

Triple Point remarks, "I hate to tell you, but you can't keep something that smells that bad a secret for very long!" He only makes the ants angrier.

Koko looks around and sees a host of army ants standing shoulder-to-shoulder marching towards them. Alarmed and afraid, Koko yells, "AIR BALL! AIR BALL!! AIR BALL!!!"

The captain of the ants commands, "C'mon! Let's get'em!"

Koko and his cousins scream as they run towards the hallway narrowly escaping the angry ants. As soon as they are in a safe place, they stop to rest.

Koko puffs, "Man, that was crazy! Triple Point, you just had to go and say something smart. Don't say anything next time!"

Triple Point looks at Koko and gasps, "Me? What did I say?!"

Preacher pants, "Hey, guys, what's done is done! We still need to find a team to play."

Koko groans, "Let's keep looking."

Chapter 6
Unkind Ladybugs

As they continue their search, they approach the sunroom. The boys are still hopeful when they see a group of round ladybugs relaxing in lawn chairs. Several ladybugs sit around a small table as they eat and play cards.

The first ladybug sips on a fruit drink and talks to the second ladybug while they scoop green chips in a veggie dip. The two ladybugs relax as they play on hand-held game consoles.

Koko turns to his cousins and says, "Let's see if they'll play with us."

Triple Point shakes his head and whispers, "Seriously, Koko? They don't really look like the basketball playing type."

Preacher elbows Triple Point and says, "C'mon, what's the worst thing that can happen?" Stringbean shrugs and replies, "Triple Point opening his mouth about them looking lazy." Triple Point counters, "Hey! I promise I won't say a word."

The boys timidly walk over to the ladybugs.

Koko smiles and politely says, "Hi, nice sunny day, isn't it? We were just passing by and wondered if you guys want to play a game of basketball with us?"

The first ladybug looks over his sunglasses at the boys and laughs, "Play basketball?... With you?... I don't think so."

Triple Point flatly says, "Basketball is fun and it's good exercise!"

The ladybugs side-eye him up and down and scowl.

The first ladybug grunts, "Are you trying to say we need to exercise?"

Stringbean smiles and replies, "No, he's just saying basketball is fun... and good exercise."

The second ladybug chokes, "Oh, please. WE'RE LADYBUGS! The only basketball games we play are on our gaming consoles. And, we win all of them."

The first ladybug looks at the boys and snootily adds, "Besides, we have bright red bodies with black dots all over us and we want our colors to beam! That's why we live in this lavish garden in the sunroom, which is the most beautiful room in the house! Why would we want to play anything with you?"

Triple Point mockingly replies, "Because clearly, you aren't doing much else?"

Koko squirms and says, "He's just kidding." He turns to Triple Point and asks, "Aren't you?"

Triple Point boldly exclaims, "NOPE!"

A third ladybug stands up and places his hand-set on the table. He gets in Triple Point's face and asks, "Are you trying to say we look like we aren't doing anything?"

Triple Point replies, "I'm not trying to say it... I AM SAYING IT."

The second ladybug walks up to Triple Point and snaps, "Just look at you. Where do I start?" She points at Koko and his cousins and says, "You look like a bad joke. Your costumes are ugly. Your shoes are ugly! In fact, everything about you is ugly!"

Stringbean replies, "These aren't costumes! They're our uniforms. We were born to play basketball."

The fourth ladybug laughs, "Yeah, yeah. Whatever! They're still ugly." He points to Stringbean's shoes and says, "Especially those big red shoes!"

The third ladybug crudely belches, "BURP... Pardon our manners. We would've offered you something to eat or drink, but we know," as he continues, "BURP... well, let's just say, you guys don't eat what we eat... BURP... As you can see, we only eat fresh organic chips and dips, AND,... BURP... drink the most nutritious, greenest fruit juices."

The fourth ladybug snickers. "I heard your folks will eat anything... living, dead, walking, crawling, running... it doesn't matter! Somebody said you guys eat shoe polish." All the ladybugs erupt in laughter.

The third ladybug hysterically laughs, "I heard last winter you guys ate the glue off the back of the wall paper." The first ladybug turns to the third ladybug and jokes, "And, I heard they ate the wallpaper when all the glue was gone." The ladybugs roll over in laughter as they slap their hands on the floor.

Unsure of what to do or say, Koko and his cousins look at each other. As the ladybugs continue to laugh at them, the boys drop their heads in shame.

The second ladybug gets up, walks over to Triple Point, and gets in his face.

"You got anything else smart to say?" she asks.

Koko edges between Triple Point and the second ladybug. He pleads, "We only stopped by to see if you wanted to play basketball."

The second ladybug, mocking Koko, whines, "'*We only stopped by to see if you wanted to play basketball.*'—If you were us, would you play basketball with you losers?"

Lucky blurts, "ABSOLUTELY!"

The second ladybug shouts, "NO, YOU WOULDN'T! AND, WE AREN'T EITHER!"

The first ladybug screams, "Take your ball and BOUNCE!" The other ladybugs chime in, "YEAH, BOUNCE!!!" The ladybugs stand side-by-side as they point to the door.

Koko says, "C'mon. Let's keep looking. We'll find someone to play with us. I really didn't want to play with them anyway." The boys turn and walk towards the sunroom door.

Once the boys exit the sunroom, Koko says, "Maybe we should get rid of our uniforms and put on something the other bugs will like."

Triple Point replies, "How 'bout YOU take off your uniform out here in the middle of nowhere and—"

Koko snaps, "Don't get mad at me! I'm just trying to think of a way to make the other bugs like us! Maybe then they'll—"

Preacher says "Koko... what else do we have to wear? Besides, there's nothing wrong with our uniforms!"

Lucky agrees, "Preacher's right! I like having my name and number on my jersey."

Koko replies, "I never said there's anything wrong with our uniforms! I'm just trying to think of a way to get them to play with us!"

Upset, Stringbean complains, "If they want to play basketball, it won't matter what we're wearing."

Koko replies, "But it does matter! They see our uniforms and—"

Triple Point, irritated, looks at Koko and utters, 'Seriously? I warned you they didn't look like they play basketball before you asked them."

Preacher says, "C'mon, guys! Let's keep looking."

The boys exit the sunroom and continue their journey down the hallway.

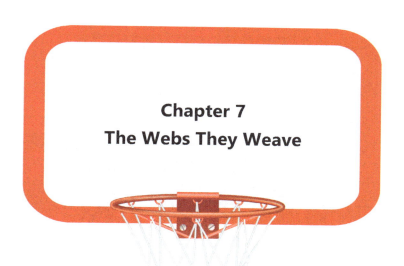

Chapter 7
The Webs They Weave

As the boys are walking down the hallway, they hear spellbinding music coming from behind a door. They see radiant beams of light, like sun rays, shine through its narrow opening. The boys peek behind the slightly cracked door and find a world of spiders busily weaving silk threads into cobwebs.

The entire wall behind the door is covered with beautiful crystal-like silk bridges connecting webs that glisten like ice castles. The vibrations of the silk strings make music that draws Koko and his cousins deeper into the room.

"Wow!" says Koko as he is drawn to the handiwork of several young spiders nearby. Stringbean stumbles over a broken boombox and a couple of skateboards on the floor beneath the webs.

"Be careful, Stringbean!" warns Preacher.

Three sly spiders become aware of the boys presence and glide down parachute-like rails from the webs and pretend to be nice to them.

The first spider politely greets them, "Hi! Can I help you?" Koko replies, "Hi, my cousins and I would like to play basketball with you guys!" The first spider snaps, "WE'RE SPIDERS! We don't play basketball!"

The second spider brags, "We make our own silk and weave it into these wonderful cobweb castles!" He looks up and points to the cobwebs. The first spider adds, "Aren't they breathtaking? We're natural-born engineers. Just look at everything we built! We're amazing, aren't we?"

Koko replies, "Well, we're natural-born basketball players! We're going to become All-stars someday!"

The spiders pause, look at each other, and giggle.

The third spider scoffs, "You??? All-stars??? Sure, you are."

"Aren't you a tad-bit too short?" sneers the first spider.

Koko politely replies, "We just hatched today! We've got plenty of time to grow."

The second spider creeps over to get a closer look at Koko and his cousins. He says, "But what are you going to do with those long antennas sticking out the middle of your foreheads? Are they going to keep growing too? You'd probably trip us up with them even if we do agree to play basketball with you."

Triple Point claps back, "If you trip over anything, it won't be our antennas. It'll be those big ol' super-duper long legs you got!" Koko elbows Triple Point and quietly whispers, "They'll never play with us if you're rude to them."

The first spider angrily responds, "You know what? I'd rather have long legs than long antennas!"

Triple Point retorts, "And I'd rather have long antennas than long legs!"

The spider counters, "Anyhow, our parents told us not to play with anyone who doesn't dress in pure silk."

The third spider points up to the glistening cobweb structures and wittily remarks, "Hey, how about this? If you guys play hide-n-seek with us in our cobweb castles, we'll play basketball with you."

The second spider winks at the third spider and agrees, "Great idea! We'll make each of you your very own pure silk jerseys to wear after we finish eating... I mean... playing hide-n-seek."

Koko considers the offer. He then replies, "Mmm,... I don't know. We know how to play basketball, but we've never played hide-n-seek before."

The first spider exclaims, "It's a fun game. We'll teach you how to play! We'll stand here, close our eyes, and slowly count to ten."

He points to an overhead cobweb near them and continues, "While we're counting down here… you guys climb up into our cobweb castles and find somewhere to hide. When we finish counting, we'll open our eyes and come search for you. Let's try it. It'll be so much fun!"

Koko eagerly agrees, "Well… that sounds like fun to me!"

The third spider adds tongue-in-cheek, "Yeah! And after you guys play hide-n-seek with us, we'll play basketball with you!"

The spiders edge closer to the boys.

Koko eagerly says, "Oh, okay… Let's play."

As Koko steps towards the nets, Triple Point glances up into one of the cobweb-castles and sees the dangling remains of several half-eaten bugs on skateboards.

Triple Point nudges Lucky, who's standing next to Koko, to look up. Lucky elbows Koko and points to the cobweb.

Lucky whispers into Koko's ear, "HEY! LOOK UP THERE!"

Koko looks up and sees the dangling remains of a bug. Open-mouthed and wide-eyed, Koko nervously backs away from the spiders. He screams with urgency, "AIR BALL! AIR BALL!! AIR BALL!!!"

As the spiders approach Koko and his cousins, they turn and run back through the narrow opening as fast as their legs will carry them.

The first spider yells, "Hey, what's wrong?! I thought you wanted to play hide-n-seek with us?"

Koko screams as he runs, "We changed our minds. Gotta go!"

The spiders run after the boys begging them to come back. The second spider pleads, "Don't leave now! We haven't gotten to the fun part yet!"

The cries of the spiders become weaker and weaker as Koko and his cousins escape down the hallway. When they no longer hear the spiders, they stop running and take a rest break. Koko wheezes, "Whew! That was close!" Lucky puffs, "Too close, if you ask me!"

Koko grumbles, "But, I thought they liked us!"

Stringbean replies, "They did... as their next meal!"

Triple Point nervously laughs. "They would've had to catch me first! I'm not going down without a fight!"

Koko snaps, "It was all your fault anyway! You had to go and make fun of their long legs!"

Triple Point looks at Koko in disbelief. He asks, "You forget what they said about our antennas?"

Preacher looks at Koko and says, "Don't blame Triple Point! What he said didn't matter. Their plans from the beginning were to trap us in their cobwebs and eat us."

Triple Point snaps at Koko, "Yeah. They talked you into playing hide-n-seek with them! And, you didn't even see those dead bugs dangling in their cobwebs. You almost got us on their menu!"

Koko states, "But they promised to play basketball with us! There has to be somebody out there who'll play with us! Let's just keep looking!"

The boys continue their journey down the hallway seeking a team to play.

Chapter 8
Pelted!

As Koko and his cousins approach a door leading to the family room, they hear flies buzzing overhead. They look up to see a fly doing handstands on a skateboard. "Wow," says Triple Point, "that's so cool."

A second fly does dance moves on a skateboard while he eats a slice of pizza. A third fly glides over the carpet on a hoverboard. He even tosses a slice of pizza to the fly doing handstands.

Koko points to a group of flies as they do dance stunts to hip-hop music blasting from their boombox. He says "Wow! Look at them."

Lucky points to a fly flying in circles recording the skaters on the floor.

Preacher elbows Koko and says, "Hey, maybe they'll play basketball with us." Lucky eagerly adds, "Yeah, I'm sure they will play with us!" Koko looks at the dancing flies and replies, "Umm... maybe. Let's see."

Koko and his cousins approach the skating flies. They stop dancing and skating and turn their music down.

Triple Point recognizes the skateboards. They look just like one he'd stumbled over under the spider webs when he glanced up into a cobweb castle. He remembers seeing the dangling remains of half-eaten bugs on skateboards.

The first fly walks up to Koko and says, "What's up?" Koko cheerfully replies, "Hi, my name is Koko... these are my cousins. Our destiny is to play basketball and we're wondering if you guys want to play a game with us?"

The first fly laughs and says to his fellow flies, "Hey! Check this out! The water heater bugs want to know if we'll play basketball with them!" He turns to Koko and grunts, "HEY, DUDE, WE'RE FLIES!"

The second fly smugly adds, "We fly and we skate. We don't fly, skate, and play basketball. We'd have to run all the way across the floor with the ball to play with you! Why would we want to do all that extra leg work?"

Triple Point jokingly replies, "Because... it's fun!"

Koko timidly asks, "How do you know where we live?"

The third fly grins, "Everybody has heard about the water heater bugs going around the house looking for someone to play basketball with."

Koko politely asks, "Well, do you want to play with us?"

The fourth fly mockingly replies, "Hmmm! Do we want to play with you?... Naw!!!... My legs already hurt from skating.' He looks at Koko and his cousins and then he looks at his fly pals. "Hey," says the fourth fly, "we all have wings. Why don't we just fly over the basket and drop the ball through the hoop?"

Stringbean counters, "That's cheating. You have to dribble or pass the ball on the court... then shoot it."

The second fly snarls, "Says who? It makes more sense for us to just fly over the basket and drop the ball through the hoop than run up and down the court dribbling, passing, and shooting."

"Yeah. Makes more sense to me, too!" sneers the third fly.

Lucky replies, "Rules are rules! You just can't up and change them because you want to!"

The second fly snaps, "Why not? Wouldn't have anything to do with the fact that you guys can't fly, would it?"

Koko declares, "We can fly. We just choose to follow the rules."

The first fly smirks, "Who're you kiddin'? Everybody knows water heater bugs can't fly!" The second fly meanly adds, "Yeah... you got long, floppy wings and their useless!" The third fly laughs, "And they're so big you can't pretend like they aren't there, either!" The flies roar in laughter.

The first fly turns to the third fly and asks, "Do you know what they call bugs with wings but can't fly?"

The third fly flaps his wings and replies, "No! What?"

The first fly points at Koko and his cousins and laughs, "LOSERS!"

All the flies swarming overhead laugh at the boys. They point at Koko and his cousins and yell, "LOSERS, LOSERS, LOSERS!"

Triple Point turns to Stringbean and mocks, "Do you know what they call flies who play hide-n-seek with spiders?"

The flies stop laughing at the boys so they can hear what Triple Point is saying to Stringbean.

Stringbean looks at Triple Point and replies, "No, what?"

Triple Point looks up, points to the flying flies, and mockingly laughs, "LUNCH, LUNCH, LUNCH!!!"

The angry flies buzz loudly over Koko and his cousins' heads.

Koko groans, "Here we go again!" He yells, "AIR BALL! AIR BALL!! AIR BALL!!!" The boys turn and run towards the door to the hallway.

The angry flies land on the carpet, pick up breadcrumbs from the floor, and pelt Koko and his cousins with them. The boys are able to dodge most of the breadcrumbs as they make their escape.

When they are safely in the hallway, they stop to rest. Koko turns to Triple Point and angrily says, "You—"

Triple Point cuts him off, "Hey, they started it. What was I supposed to do? I'm not going to let them joke me out like that!"

Koko shakes his head in frustration. He tells Triple Point, "We'll never find anyone to play with us if you keep talking!"

Triple Point replies, "I promise I'm not saying anything else."

Preacher shrugs and sighs, "Let's just keep looking."

Chapter 9
All That Glitters

As the boys walk quietly down the hallway, they approach the bathroom. They peek around the door and see several silverfish standing near the toilet bowl.

Two silverfish stare at themselves in the mirrored wall as they pose by the toilet bowl base. A third silverfish stands on the floor near the toilet as he admires himself in a hand-held mirror.

Lucky elbows Koko and whispers, "Hey, do you want to see if they'll play basketball with us?" Koko gleefully replies, "What do we have to lose?"

The boys approach the silverfish.

Koko bubbly says, "Hi, my cousins and I would like to challenge you guys to a game of basketball." The first silverfish looks at Koko and his cousins and sighs. He turns away totally ignoring them.

Koko speaks a little louder, "Excuse me. My name is Koko and these are my cousins, We'd like to challenge you guys to a game of basketball." The third silverfish stops looking at himself in his mirror and replies, "You know, we heard you the first time. We hoped you'd take the hint and stop talking to us. WE'RE SILVERFISH! We don't play basketball."

Triple Point shakes his head and whispers to Stringbean, "Why am I not surprised!" Koko gives Triple Point a disapproving glance.

The second silverfish looks at Triple Point and snaps, "You know what else? I don't like you, so I'm just going to act like you aren't here."

The third silverfish says, "In case you haven't noticed, our bodies are silver, slender, and perfectly fashioned for the finer things in life. As you can see, we're the best-looking insects in the entire universe."

The first silverfish remarks, "Everybody knows we look good, don't we?" Stringbean politely replies, "We just hatched this morning. If you say you're the best-looking insects, who're we to say you're not? I just know I'm handsome."

The first Silverfish looks at Stringbean and says, "Wrong answer! Have you any social standing?" Koko answers, "Of course we have social standing! Look at how tall Stringbean and Triple Point are when they stand up straight." Stringbean and Triple Point stand on their toes with their heads held high to appear taller.

The silverfish look at each other and explode in laughter.

The second silverfish shakes his head and says, "You boys aren't too smart either, are you? Where do you live?" Preacher proudly announces, "We live in the laundry room in the basement under the water heater!"

The third silverfish coughs as if he's choking. "Surely you're kidding?! You live under that dank, moldy water heater... IN THE LAUNDRY ROOM! The basement... that's the worst place in the whole house to live," he shrieks.

The second silverfish squeals, "Ewww! How utterly disgusting! You boys have a lot of nerve asking silverfish to play basketball with you! Look around you! We live behind this beautiful toilet bowl in this spotless bathroom while you live under that nasty, filthy water heater in the laundry room... IN THE BASEMENT of all places! Play with you? Not going to happen!"

Stringbean angrily replies, "We may live under the water heater in the laundry room in the basement, but it's not nasty and we don't live in filth."

Lucky adds, "Yeah, we don't live in filth."

The third silverfish laughs unkindly and says, "Yes, you do! Where do you think dust bunnies come from?"

Lucky responds, "Our water heater doesn't have dust bunnies!"

The second silverfish points at Lucky's feet and meanly says, "Yes it does! Look at your shoes. Where do you think that dust came from?"

Koko and his cousins look down at their shoes and see white, powdery spider-web dust. Lucky replies defensively, "It didn't come from under the water heater. It came from the spider webs behind the door down the hall."

The third silverfish laughs, "Sure it did! Just don't leave any of your water heater dust bunnies in here!"

The first silverfish points to the door and yells, "Take yourselves and your crusty-dusty little ball out of our clean bathroom... NOW!"

The second silverfish screeches in disgust, "MAKE SURE YOU DON'T TOUCH ANYTHING ON YOUR WAY OUT! BYE!"

The third silverfish angrily yells, "AND, DON'T DROP ANY COOTIES AS YOU LEAVE!"

Stringbean turns to look at the third silverfish and states angrily, "Cooties??? Excuse you!"

The third silverfish grimaces and says, "Excuse ME?... Excuse YOU! Don't act like you don't know what I'm talking about... look at you... you're covered in cooties."

The first silverfish scowls, "Yeah. You filthy little pests need to crawl back under the water heater where you belong and stay there!"

Koko and his cousins turn and walk away. He tells his cousins, "C'mon, let's go. We would've beat them anyway!" The boys keep their antennas high as they walk back towards the hallway entrance.

Stringbean turns to Triple Point and heatedly asks, "Why didn't you say something?"

Triple Point angrily replies, "WHAT? When I say something, Koko says I shouldn't have said anything. When I don't say anything, you say I should have said something! MAN! What do you want from me? I told you I was keeping my mouth closed!"

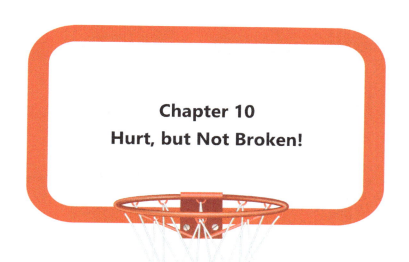

Chapter 10
Hurt, but Not Broken!

Once the boys are far enough away from the silverfish that they can't be heard, Koko's cousins turn their attention to him. Triple Point angrily says, "Well, Captain Koko, I've had enough of looking for another team to play!" Lucky, Stringbean, and Preacher look down and nod their heads in agreement.

Koko drops his head in defeat and replies, "Okay, let's go home." While they walk slowly back to the laundry room, each of them is lost in his own thoughts. One by one, their antennas droop as tears stream down their cheeks.

The boys are unaware that Grandpa Jack followed them the whole journey. He knows everything that happened and how they were treated. When they are close to the laundry room and Grandpa Jack knows they will make it home safely, he takes a short cut back to the water heater. He gets home a few minutes before the boys.

When they arrive home, Grandpa Jack is reclining in his chair and reading his jTab newsfeed. He looks up and sees their sad expressions and drooping antennas. The boys sit on the floor around his chair.

Grandpa Jack says, "Back so soon. How did everything go?"

The boys look down in silence as they wait for one of them to say something... anything. Finally, Koko mutters, "No one would play basketball with us!"

"Yeah, and they made fun of everything about us. The ants said we're lazy. The ladybugs called us ugly," whimpers Preacher.

Koko adds, "And, the spiders. Don't forget the spiders. They said they couldn't play with us because we weren't dressed in pure silk."

Triple Point turns to Koko and exclaims, "You didn't get the big picture. They tried to trick us into playing hide-n-seek with them in their webs so they could trap us and eat us!

Lucky angrily adds, "Don't leave out the flies... they called us losers because we have wings but can't fly! They even threw breadcrumbs at us!"

Stringbean mockingly adds, "And the silverfish called us disgusting pests... They even said we have dust bunnies and cooties because we live in the nasty laundry room. Can you believe that?"

Koko looks at Grandpa Jack and asks, "This is a big house. Why can't we move to another room?"

Grandpa Jack looks at Koko and replies, "There's nothing wrong with where we live. What you need to understand is it's not where you start in life that counts, it's where you finish and who you become along the way."

Angry and frustrated, Stringbean responds, "But nobody likes us! Why couldn't we've been born silverfish or ladybugs or spiders or ants or even flies?"

Koko tearfully adds, "He's right. We'd be better off if we'd never hatched!"

Stringbean blurts, "Yeah!"

Lucky angrily clenches his fists and yells, "I hate them. I hate all of them!"

Grandpa Jack frowns and shakes his head. He looks at Lucky and says, "Hate... that's a strong word. You may feel angry... for a little while, but hate? NO!"

Lucky looks at Grandpa Jack and cries, "You weren't there. We were kind to them... but they were mean to us!"

Grandpa Jack responds, "I followed you and was there every step of your journey. You boys just hatched today. Do you think I'd let you wander around this big house by yourselves? I was there and I'll always be there until I know you are old enough to take care of yourselves. I'm your grandfather. I love you and I'll always be close by to protect you."

The weeping boys look at Grandpa Jack and see tears in his eyes. They jump to their feet, run to hug him, and tell him, "We love you, Grandpa." Grandpa Jack hugs the boys and tells them, "Always remember I love you more!" He motions for them to sit back down as he removes his spectacles and wipes his eyes.

Grandpa Jack puts his spectacles back on and turns his attention to Lucky. "When you think about what the other bugs said and how they treated you, how do you feel?"

Lucky angrily replies, "I want to hurt them like they hurt me."

Grandpa Jack prods further, "But, how do you feel?" Lucky lowers his head and quietly answers, "I feel like maybe there's something wrong with me. I feel really bad."

Grandpa Jack glances at each of the boys. They all look sad. "When I was your age, someone said something really mean to me. I was hurt and felt like there was something wrong with me. I was ashamed of myself. My coach told me, *'Sticks and stones may break my bones, but words can never hurt me!'* But do you know what?" he asks.

"What?" replies the boys.

"Words do hurt. And that's one thing you really need to remember: Words. Are. Powerful. Once they are spoken, they can't be unspoken. Be careful what you say to others, especially when you are angry or tired."

The boys answer, "Yes, sir!"

"Now, I want each of you to think about the bugs who were mean to you today. Do you think they are thinking about you or what they said to you right now? Do you think they are feeling hurt or bad?" asks Grandpa Jack, " I'd say they probably aren't."

The boys shift as they look at each other not sure how to feel. Triple Point angrily shakes his head and explains, "You just don't get it—"

Grandpa Jack raises one of his hands to stop Triple Point from saying anything else. He calmly but firmly states, "I do get it! Their words hurt you! Words can be so hurtful that they make you sick. I get it, but what I need you to get is that hurtful words only hurt if YOU give those words power. I'm not saying ignore what they said or pretend it didn't happen. What I am saying is to decide if what they said is true or not. If it's true, you've got to deal with it. If it's not true, then it's nonsense that you shake off and keep moving forward. Once you figure out what to do, you can let go of the hurt and anger that some words cause and forgive them. If you don't, you'll become bitter and that bitterness will grow into hate. Hate will only hurt you. The sooner you forgive whoever hurt you, the sooner you'll feel better."

The boys settle down but still look angry. Triple Point clinches his hands into fists and says, "I'd feel better if I had punched one of them."

Grandpa Jack shakes his head and replies, "Anger makes us want to fight. But what would happen if they punch you back? Fighting and violence only lead to more fighting and violence. Nothing good comes from that response. I know it sounds hard but you'll only feel better when you forgive whoever hurts you."

The boys look at Grandpa Jack as if he doesn't understand how they feel. Seeing the expressions on their faces Grandpa Jack says, "Okay, it's the perfect time for a little experiment."

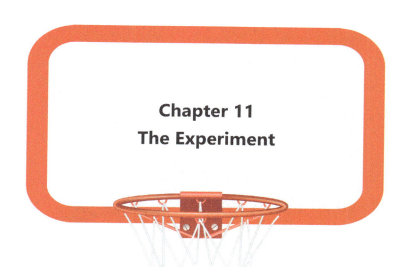

Chapter 11
The Experiment

Grandpa Jack goes to the table and picks up a bowl of candy balls neatly wrapped in colorful cellophane. He carries the bowl over to the boys and says, "Take a piece of candy and eat it."

Each of the boys takes a piece of candy from the bowl, unwraps it, and puts it in his mouth. Immediately, they spit the candy back into the wrappers.

Koko exclaims, "Ewww! That's gross! I thought you said you love us! Are you punishing all of us for what Triple Point said?"

Grandpa Jack smiles and replies, "Yes, I do love you. And, no, you're not being punished." He returns the bowl to the table and gives each of the boys water to drink.

While this is going on, the five recently-hatched girl bugs tip-toe into the room through the door leading to Coach Lovelady's bedroom. They sit on the floor next to Coach Lovelady. They are also dressed in Long Shots uniforms.

Grandpa Jack firmly declares, "Hurt and anger are like those sour, bitter candies. You put them in your mouth and they leave a bitter taste. That bitter taste is like hate. Even after you spit the sour balls out, you need water to wash away the bitter taste. To get rid of the hurt and anger that leads to bitter feelings of hate, you have to forgive them."

Preacher looks at Grandpa Jack with a puzzled expression and asks, "Forgive them? What do you mean forgive them?"

Grandpa Jack replies, "I mean you have to choose to let go of feeling like you need to hurt them back for hurting you. That means, when you see them again, you'll be able to treat them with kindness."

The boys look at each other with disbelief on their faces. Then they look at Grandpa Jack in shock.

Koko asks, "You mean... we have to like them?"

Grandpa Jack firmly states, "No, that's not what I mean. But you do have to treat them the way you'd want them to treat you! In our family, we live by The Golden Rule: 'Treat others the way you would want them to treat you!' So, if you see one of the bugs who was mean to you in need of help and you can help them, you help them."

Preacher perks up, raises his hand, and asks, "Oh! Does that mean they'll be kind to us, too?"

Grandpa Jack looks sad and replies, "No. They'll probably still be mean to you. And, they'll probably never ask you to forgive them. That brings us to my next point. You don't forgive someone who hurts you because they deserve to be forgiven. You forgive them because you deserve to be free from anger and hate. You can't control what they say or how they treat you, but you can control how you respond. They don't get to determine who you are... **YOU** do. Always be kind."

Grandpa Jack takes off his spectacles, wipes them with a tissue, and puts them back on. He looks lovingly at each of the boys. He says, "Now, I want each of you to take a moment and think about what happened today and tell me what you learned."

The boys' antennae begin to perk up as they each reflect on their own thoughts.

Chapter 12
Think About It!

Grandpa Jack gives the boys a few minutes to reflect on their experiences. "Let's start with you, Lucky," says Grandpa Jack.

Lucky smiles and says, "I learned that not everyone is going to be kind to me... no matter how kind I am to them... but it's better to forgive them than stay angry and hate them."

Grandpa Jack nods his head and says, "Stringbean?" Stringbean says, "I learned that no matter how good I play basketball or that I'm the most handsome member on our team—"

Triple Point whispers under his breath, "You wish!"

Looking annoyed at Triple Point, Stringbean continues, "I can't change what anyone else thinks or says about me, but I don't have to accept it as my truth." He laughs mockingly and adds, "And that, my dear cousins, is what 'Your Handsomeness' learned!"

Grandpa Jack looks at Triple Point and nods. Triple Point stands to his feet and states, "I learned that not everyone is going to like me... and that's okay... but, spiders... stay away from them. They'll pretend to be your friends so they can trap you into their webs and eat you!" He turns to Stringbean, bows, and sits back down. The boys laugh.

Triple Point jumps to his feet for a second time and adds, "Oh! And one more thing! I could've totally taken down that third spider!" Koko, Stringbean, Preacher, and Lucky look at each other in disbelief and burst into laughter. Stringbean jokingly replies, "Yeah, right! You ran over all of us getting away from them! We couldn't see anything but the dust trail you left behind!" The other boys laugh and nod in agreement.

Grandpa Jack turns to asks, "Preacher, what did you learn?" Preacher looks thoughtfully at Grandpa Jack and replies, "I learned to appreciate my ability to run fast when things get dangerous! And,... I have a family I can run home to when things get too rough."

Grandpa Jack nods and says, "Koko? It's on you." Koko looks seriously at each of his cousins. He then looks at Grandpa Jack and responds, "Well, I learned we should always stick together... and why the Golden Rule is important to our family. I'd never want to be mean to anyone because it hurt when the other bugs were mean to us."

Grandpa Jack removes his spectacles and dabs his eyes. He looks proudly at the boys and says, "You boys learned some valuable lessons and I'm very proud of you. Now, let me tell you some interesting things about our family you can be proud of too!" The boys' antennas perk straight up.

Grandpa Jack proudly tells them, "You come from a family of strong bugs. We can live three months without food and a whole month without water!" Stringbean reacts, "Wow!! That's good to know."

Grandpa Jack goes on to tell them, "And guess what?... If you lose a leg, you'll just grow another one!"

Koko jumps to his feet and exclaims, "WHAT?... Grow a new leg? Wow!!!"

"Wait, that doesn't mean you go out and break your leg off just to grow a new one. It'll still hurt!" warns Grandpa Jack.

The boys burst into laughter.

Grandpa Jack explains, "We have thousands of different types of bugs in our family. And, we live all over the world."

The boys smile and their antennas perk completely up.

Triple Point responds, "Wow! That's awesome!"

Grandpa Jack smiles and adds "By the way, some of our cousins DO fly." Preacher gasps, "For real?!!!"

"Yes!" adds Grandpa Jack, "Even bug spray can't stop us! If all of us males disappear, the females will just keep laying female eggs."

The boys look at each other with confused expressions. They then look at Grandpa Jack.

Preacher asks, "Females? What are females?"

Chapter 13
Meet the Girls

Grandpa Jack chuckles and replies, "I thought you'd never ask! Turn around and meet your female, or rather, girl cousins. They hatched about the same time you did on the other side of the water heater. They live near their gym with your aunt." Grandpa Jack motions for Coach Lovelady to join him. She walks up to the front of the room and gives him a hug.

Coach Lovelady turns to the girls and says, "This is my father and your grandfather, Grandpa Jack." She turns to Grandpa Jack and says, "And these beautiful and amazingly talented girls are your granddaughters."

Coach Lovelady starts, "This is Kookie #2, SUGAR #4, KANDI #6, TEA #8, and GRACE #10, the youngest in the group. Kookie is our team captain."

Grandpa Jack walks over to the girls and hugs them. "Wow," he says, "We've been waiting for you to hatch. You girls are absolutely beautiful!"

The girls stand tall, look at each other, and smile.

Grandpa Jack says, "This is Koko #1, Preacher #3, Lucky #5, Triple Point #7, and Stringbean #9. Koko is the captain of the boys' team."

Coach Lovelady greets the boys with hugs and kisses. She tells them, "I'm glad to see you made it back home safely."

The boys greet their girl cousins with high-fives and fist bumps.

Kandi looks at Grandpa Jack and asks, "How did we all get to be cousins?" Grandpa Jack replies, "Because all of your mothers were sisters."

Kandi ponders, "Oh, okay, I guess that makes sense."

Kookie fist bumps Koko and says "What's up, Captain Koko?" She picks up a ball from the corner and passes it to Tea.

Triple Point eagerly replies, "Sure."

"We heard you're looking for a team to play basketball with. Want to play with us?" asks Tea.

Sugar teasingly says, "I have to warn you... we'll beat you. We'll make shots you never saw coming."

Stringbean mockingly replies, "Yeah, right! And we've never missed a basket!"

Sugar gives Stringbean serious side-eye. She turns to Grace and asks, "Did he just challenge us?" Grace giggles, "Sounds like he did to me. He has no idea."

"Hey, guys, it's time for lunch. Wash your hands before you sit down to eat. You can play basketball after you're done," says Grandpa Jack.

The cousins eat their lunch as quickly as they can.

"Mmm, that was good." exclaims Koko. "It sure was," agrees the other cousins. Once their dishes are washed and put away, Koko picks up a ball and smiles teasingly at the girls. He passes the ball around Sugar to Triple Point. Kookie steals the ball from Triple Point and passes it to Tea.

As Tea dribbles and passes the ball to Kookie, she playfully laughs, "We WERE going to go easy on you guys, seeing how tired you are from your journey today—"

"But now we've got to show you who's the boss!" adds Kookie. She tries to pass the ball to Grace but Triple Point jumps and catches it mid-air. Triple Point grins, "Yeah, right!" He dribbles the ball and is about to throw an overhead pass to Stringbean.

Coach Lovelady claps her hands loudly. She softly but firmly tells them, "We don't play ball in the house! Take it to the gym."

The cousins reply, "Yes, ma'am!"

Koko turns to face his cousins and says, "C'mon guys, let's go to the gym." He turns to Grandpa Jack and asks, "Can we go?"

Grandpa Jack replies, "Sure." The boys and girls run towards the door.

Coach Lovelady frowns and says, "No running in the house!"

The cousins giggle softly and reply, "Yes, ma'am!" They hurriedly tiptoe across the floor to the door and make a mad dash to the boys' gym.

Coach Lovelady and Grandpa Jack gather their jTabs and follow them.

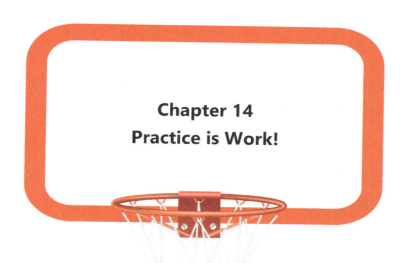

Chapter 14
Practice is Work!

Grandpa Jack and Coach Lovelady enter the gym and sit at the coach's table. They set up plays for practice while the cousins pass and shoot balls among each other.

Coach Lovelady blows her whistle to call them to the coach's table. Grandpa Jack tells them, "Before you practice, always begin with stretches and warm ups."

Koko groans, "We've been running and walking all day. Can't we just play with the girls now and start with stretches and warm-ups tomorrow?" Grandpa Jack gives Koko a very stern look and says, "No. Start with arm and leg stretches first. Then, follow the stretches with waist twists and lunges. After that, do ten laps around the gym."

Koko frowns and stomps as he walks away. All of his cousins turn and stare at him. Sugar whispers to Kookie, "Uh, oh! He's in t-r-o-u-b-l-e!" Speechless, Coach Lovelady glances at Koko and turns to Grandpa Jack.

Grandpa Jack looks sternly at Koko and says, "Behavior like that will not be tolerated from you or any of your cousins. You will not disrespect me or your aunt. When we tell you to do something, you either do it, or explain to us why you can't do it. Stomping, murmuring, talking back, raising your voice, or anything that closely looks like disrespect is unacceptable. Have I made myself clear!"

Koko drops his head in shame and says, "Yes, sir."

Coach Lovelady looks at Koko and his cousins as she tells them, "It goes back to the Golden Rule: 'Treat others the way you want them to treat you.' No one wants to be disrespected so don't disrespect anyone else. Understood?" Koko and his cousins reply, "Yes, ma'am!"

Preacher moves next to Koko and whispers in his ear, "You need to apologize." Koko nods, "I know."

Koko walks over to Grandpa Jack and says, "I'm sorry!"

Grandpa Jack replies, "I accept your apology. Don't let it happen again." He adjusts Koko's cap, "Now do as you were told."

Koko runs back to his teammates and says, "Come on, let's do our stretches and warm ups." He leads his teammates through everything as Grandpa Jack directed.

The girls completed their stretches and warm ups and join the boys as they run laps around the gym.

Grandpa Jack signals both teams to the boys' end of the court. "We've decided to let you practice together so all of you can learn some of the rules of basketball at the same time.

Triple Point asks, "Can we play just one game with the girls before we leave?" Sugar jokes, "Man, you guys really want to get beat today, don't you?" Triple Point shakes his head and smiles as he stands next to Sugar. He realizes how tall he is over her.

Tea looks at Triple Point and snaps, "What's so funny?!" Triple Point chuckles and replies, "Nothing... nothing at all!"

Grandpa Jack and Coach Lovelady run the cousins through dribbling, shooting, and passing drills. They show them how to do layups, basic footwork, and ball handling. Grandpa Jack and Coach Lovelady try to make sure that each player learns ways to improve their skills and avoid fouling players on the other team.

Grandpa Jack states, "Okay, we'll let you play a five-minute game before we break for dinner. Coach Lovelady will keep track of the score and the clock. Are you ready?" The cousins yell, "YES."

Kookie and Koko meet Grandpa Jack center court for the jump ball. Koko tips the ball to Stringbean. The boys dribble and pass the ball between Lucky, Stringbean, and Preacher before Triple Point attempts to make a basket. Kandi blocks him. Triple Point passes the ball to Koko. As Koko dribbles the ball, Tea scoops under his arm and steals it. She passes it to Sugar. Stringbean tries to block Sugar but she pushes around him, shoots the ball, and scores the first basket.

Grandpa Jack grimaces and blows his whistle calling a timeout. He tells the boys to keep their eyes on the ball and pay attention to who's guarding them. He also tells Triple Point not to assume that because he is taller than the girls, they can't shoot over or around him.

Coach Lovelady meets with the excited girls and gives them high fives. She tells them to keep playing hard, but remember to have fun. She blows her whistle and the cousins return to the court.

There are now three minutes and thirty-two seconds left on the clock. The score is 2-0 in favor of the girls. The boys have control of the ball. Stringbean dribbles the ball down the court. After he crosses the mid-court line, he passes it to Triple Point. Triple Point dribbles the ball and tries to make a shot. He is heavily covered by Tea. Triple Point passes it to Stringbean.

Stringbean dribbles and passes the ball to Preacher. Preacher passes it to Triple Point. Triple Point fakes a pass to Lucky. He shoots the ball from the three-point arc, and scores a three-point basket.

Coach Lovelady blows her whistle calling a timeout for the girls. The score is now 2-3 in favor of the boys. There are two minutes and forty-one seconds left on the clock.

Coach Lovelady warns the girls to expect the unexpected when it comes to fake shots. She tells them, "Keep your eyes on the ball and look for any and every opportunity to steal it."

Kookie says, "They're tired and we're not. Let's run them until they start making mistakes. Then, it'll be easier to steal the ball." The girls nod.

Grandpa Jack blows his whistle and the cousins return to the court. The girls have possession of the ball. Grace drives the ball down the court and passes it to Kandi. Kandi dribbles the ball and passes it to Tea. She runs around Lucky and passes the ball to Kookie. Kookie fakes a jump shot and passes the ball to Sugar. Triple Point tries to block Sugar, but she dances around him and passes the ball to Tea.

"HEY!" shrieks Triple Point.

Tea dribbles the ball twice and tries to make a shot. Lucky blocks her. She passes the ball to Kandi. But, Kandi is blocked by Stringbean. She passes the ball to Grace. Koko blocks Grace, so she passes the ball to Sugar.

Sugar, who is now in the three-point zone, dances around Triple Point and shoots the ball. She makes a basket and scores three points for the girls. The score is now 5-3 in favor of the girls.

Grandpa Jack blows his whistle and calls another timeout. The boys flop down on a bleacher near him.

Triple Point admits, "I'm tired. I didn't know how tired I was until now." Koko declares, "Me, too! And we still have almost two minutes left to play."

Grandpa Jack asks, "Do you want to finish the game tomorrow?" "YES!" answer the boys.

Grandpa Jack walks over to Coach Lovelady and explains to her what's going on. He returns to the bleachers and tells the boys, "We'll finish the game tomorrow after practice. You boys take a shower and relax. When you're done, you can go help the girls prepare dinner." The boys reply "Yes, sir."

As they head to the showers, Triple Point says, "I'll be ready for Sugar tomorrow." Stringbean jokes, "So she can wipe the floor with you like she did today? Why don't you just admit she's good?"

Triple Point adds, "I'm tired, that's all."

Stringbean teases, "Right! Whatever you say, buddy, whatever you say!" Triple Point, slightly angry by Stringbean's teasing, playfully elbows him.

PART 2
THE NEIGHBORHOOD FRENEMIES

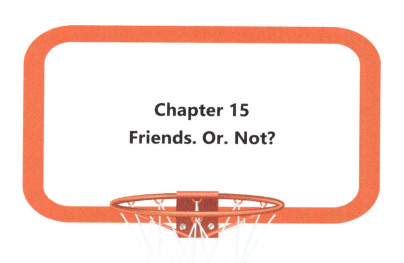

Chapter 15
Friends. Or. Not?

When Koko and his cousins leave the gym, they run into a group of young, flashy-dressed bugs hanging around in the breezeway that leads to their home. The group stops talking to each other and turn to stare at the boys as they walk by.

Koko politely says, "Hi! I'm Koko." He turns to his cousins and adds, "These are my cousins, Lucky, Stringbean, Triple Point, and Preacher." He tucks his ball under his arm and reaches out for a fist-bump.

The mean bugs look at Koko's fist and turn up their noses. Koko drops his hand unsure of how to respond.

Too Cool steps away from Koko and his cousins. He frowns as if he smells a bad odor. "I'm Too Cool. My friends call me T.C.! This is my crew—Trouble, Excus, Sorri, Patsy and Mony," snorts Too Cool. Trouble and the rest of his crew circle the boys.

Too Cool points at Koko and asks, "What trash can did you get those get-ups from?"

Triple Point replies, "These aren't get-ups! They're our basketball uniforms."

Too Cool cocks his head and fakes earnestness, "Okay, what trash can did you get those ugly uniforms from?"

"The same trash can you got your attitude from!" replies Triple Point.

Trouble gets in Triple Point's face and asks, "Do you know who you're talking to?"

Koko edges himself between Trouble and Triple Point as Stringbean pulls Triple Point to the side.

Koko nervously laughs, "Hey! He's just kidding."

Preacher rambles, "Yeah! He's kidding, aren't you Triple Point? Triple Point, always there with the jokes. He—"

Triple Point replies firmly, "**No! I'm not kidding**!"

Koko elbows Triple Point and says, "We were born to play basketball. What were you guys born to do?"

Too Cool and his crew glance at each other and then stare at the boys. Too Cool arrogantly replies, "We were born to be cool!"

Preacher curiously asks, "What do you mean, you were 'born to be cool'?"

Patsy snobbishly replies, "It means **we are** the **'IT'** group. We define what it means to be popular. The world gives and we take. We say whether you're **IN** or **OUT**!"

Trouble steps back and spins in a complete circle. He boasts, "We only wear designer clothes and live the 'Everybody wants to be me!' life. Everyone who is anyone wants to be cool like us!"

Koko timidly asks, "Well... a-are we cool?"

Excus and Sorri shout, "NO!"

Stringbean, seemingly unfazed, asks, "Assuming we want to be "cool", what do we have to do?"

Mony smugly replies, "Did you hear anything he said? You have to hang out with us!"

Preacher prods further, "I still don't understand what you mean."

Trouble spouts, "Our friends get to hang out with all the cool bugs that live under this water heater and do all the 'IN' things. If you aren't our friends, you have no friends at all!"

Mony pulls out his wallet and brags, "It takes money to buy cool things. Money won't make you cool, **but it will buy you cool friends!**"

Patsy nods her head and says, "If you don't dress in designer clothes, follow us, and do what we do, you can forget about ever being cool!"

Koko says, "Well, T.C.—" Too Cool's crew stops and stares at Koko.

Sorri points her phone at Koko and snaps, "What did you just call him?! We can call him T.C., but you can't! It's friends only!"

Excus adds, "And, you're not our friends."

Koko pleads, "Can we be your friends?"

Sorri laughs, "Assuming we even want you as friends, you have to do whatever T.C. says. First, lose those ugly costumes!" She points at Lucky's shoes, "**And,** get rid of those horrible shoes."

Triple Point tells them, "These are our uniforms. They stay!"

Too Cool gives in, "Whatever! You won't be able to hang out with us and dress like that for long. You'll eventually want to dress like us. Aside from that, whatever I say goes. I do the thinking and talking. I lead, you follow. You ask no questions and I don't have to explain anything to you. Your loyalty is always to me. You answer to me and only to me.

If I laugh, you laugh. When I stop laughing, you stop laughing."

Too Cool points to himself and then to Koko. "We'll be your family. What's yours is mine. When you need something, ask me. Now, if you're IN, let's roll!"

Too Cool and Trouble step away from Koko and his cousins. They wait for them to make their decision.

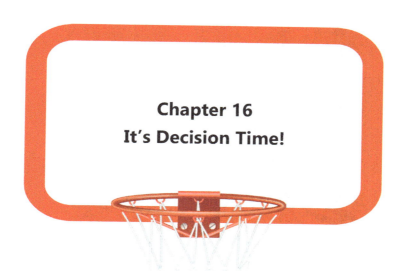

Chapter 16
It's Decision Time!

Koko and his cousins huddle together and talk about Too Cool's offer to become part of their cool group. Koko wants to be in their group but his cousins think it's a bad idea.

Koko pressures them saying, "Well,... hey, why not? Grandpa Jack said it's good to have friends."

Preacher replies, "That's not what he said. He told us we should be friendly to everyone."

Lucky adds, "Preacher is right. I don't think hanging out with Too Cool is a good idea."

Stringbean and Triple Point nod in agreement.

Too Cool walks over and stops the boys before they make a decision. He throws his arm around Koko's shoulder and pulls him away from his cousins. Too Cool tells Koko, "Man, forget them. They'll never be cool!"

Preacher steps towards Koko and whispers to him, "Are you sure you want to go with them?" Koko replies, "Yes, I really want them to like me."

Triple Point, Stringbean, and Lucky talk among themselves. "There's something not right about them," whispers Triple Point. Stringbean softly replies, "Let's not forget, Grandpa Jack told us to go help the girls make dinner. He didn't say anything about going anywhere with anyone else."

Preacher joins Triple Point, Stringbean and Lucky. Preacher shakes his head and says, "I tried to tell Koko we shouldn't go with them, but he's going. What are we going to do?"

Triple Point sighs, "I don't think we should go. But Grandpa Jack did tell us to always stay together."

Lucky adds, "We're going to be in trouble either way."

Preacher agrees, "He is the captain, but going with them is not a good choice. Let's just stay together for now. If something else comes up that we don't want to do, we'll leave. Maybe Koko will leave with us!"

Koko follows Too Cool and his crew. The boys reluctantly follow Koko.

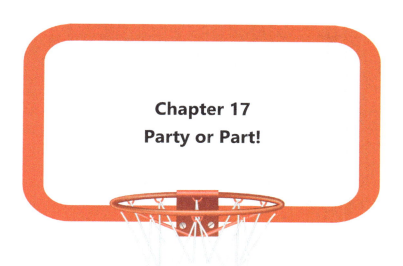

Chapter 17
Party or Part!

Too Cool and his crew lead Koko and his cousins to a closet where a party is already underway. Loud music and a weird-smelling mist greet them at the door. They immediately cover their noses with their hands.

Preacher chokes, "Ewww, gross! What's that smell?"

Triple Point coughs and gags, "Is something burning?"

Lucky wheezes, "I can hardly breathe. I'm not going in there!"

Stringbean calls out to Lucky, "What did you say? I can't understand a word you're saying. The music is too loud! It's making my ears hurt!"

Preacher turns to Koko as he struggles to breathe. He gasps, "I've had enough. I'm out of here!" Lucky, Stringbean, and Triple Point nod their heads in agreement.

Koko says, "Come on, guys. We're here now. Let's at least give it a try. We may never get another chance to be cool! What's the worst thing that can happen?"

Triple Point shakes his head and tells Koko, "No! You stay if you want to, but we're going home!" Koko's cousins shake their heads as they prepare to leave him at the party.

Too Cool walks over to Koko and tells him, "Let those losers leave. You don't need them anymore. We're your family now!"

Trouble angrily adds, "They're not cool like you. They'll never be 'IN!'"

Excus, Sorri, and Patsy chime, "Bye, losers!" Mony looks at them in disgust.

Koko finally speaks up, "They're not losers! They're my cousins."

Trouble laughs, "We're your cousins, now."

Preacher, Lucky, Stringbean, and Triple Point shake their heads, turn, and leave.

Koko follows Too Cool and his crew into the closet. A group of older bugs are dancing and drinking something from red cups.

Excus, Sorri and Patsy go off in a corner and get red cups for themselves and their crew.

Patsy hands a red cup to Koko. He smells it and decides not to drink it. Trouble whispers something to Too Cool.

Too Cool walks over to Koko and stands next to him. He pushes the cup up towards Koko's mouth. "**Drink it!**" presses Too Cool. "You're not going to make me look bad in front of my friends."

Koko can't see what's in the red cup because the closet is too dark. He asks, "What's this?"

Trouble replies, "Didn't you understand the rules? Don't ask questions. Just **drink it** like Too Cool said!"

Koko puts the cup to his mouth but decides he really doesn't want to drink whatever is in it. He stammers, "I don't want—"

All the bugs in the closet are now looking at Koko. Too Cool bitterly whispers into Koko's ear, "**Drink it or leave!** You think I'm going to let you make me look bad in front of my friends?"

Koko looks straight into Too Cool's angry eyes and suddenly becomes afraid. He finally understands that Too Cool is not a nice bug.

Koko turns around and hands the cup back to Patsy. He turns to Too Cool and says, "Thank you for inviting me to this party, but I don't belong here. I'm going to find my real cousins."

Too Cool shrugs and says, "Whatever!" He and his friends turn their backs to Koko and continue partying.

Koko walks to the door and exits the closet.

Chapter 18
Oops!

As Triple Point, Preacher, Lucky and Stringbean walk home, they discuss the mess they are in and how they're going to explain things to Grandpa Jack.

Triple Point says, "I wish we'd never stopped to talk to Too Cool and his crew."

Lucky says, "Actually, we didn't stop to talk to them. They stopped us."

Preacher responds, "It's too late to change anything now. We have a bigger problem—what we're going to tell Grandpa Jack when he sees Koko isn't with us."

Stringbean slaps his face in his hands and yelps, "Oh, No! I hadn't thought about that! We'd better think of something, quick!"

Triple Point says, "I think we'd best slow down and come up with something to say."

"How about we tell him the truth. He probably followed us anyway," replies Preacher as he looks around to see if Grandpa Jack is watching them.

With lowered heads and antennas drooping, they walk home at a snail's pace.

Preacher hears chatter in the distance and looks up to see Kookie, Kandi, Tea, Sugar, and Grace walking towards them.

Preacher perks up and says, "Hey! It's the girls! Maybe they'll know what to do."

Kookie walks up to Preacher to give him a high five. His arm goes up slightly then flops back down. She looks at him and notices his sad face. She says, "What's up? We just left Grandpa Jack a few minutes ago. He said you were supposed to come over and help us make dinner…"

Grace looks around and asks, "Hey! Where's Koko?" Triple Point acts surprised and jokingly asks, "Koko?! Who's that?"

Kookie asks, "Seriously! Where's Koko?"

Preacher replies, "He's... we left him at a party with Too Cool."

Grace stares at him with wide-eyes and replies, "You're kidding, right?"

Triple Point looks at Grace and asks, "Oh! So, you know them?"

Tea says, "We know **of** them. They're everywhere. Trouble and his twin sisters—Excus and Sorri—you CAN say we've heard about them."

Kandi shutters, "Don't forget Patsy and Mony. She agrees with whatever they say and he's always broke. Did you say something about a party?... With them? What were you thinking?"

"They're boys! They probably weren't thinking!" adds Tea. Grace turns to Tea and says, "Let's not pour salt on their wounds. They already feel bad enough." Stringbean lowers his head and responds, "She's right. We didn't think he'd choose them over us."

Kookie looks at the four boys and asks, "What **are** you going to tell Grandpa Jack? How are you going to explain to him you left Koko at a party with Too Cool? He knows them, too."

"Hmmm, let's think about this for a minute," ponders Sugar as she begins to pace back and forth in front of the group. She places one hand under her chin and raises and lowers her head as if she's thinking really hard.

The girls step back and look at Sugar unsure of what she will say. Tea shakes her head and rolls her eyes up.

Sugar's antennas shoot straight up and twitch up and down. Kookie whispers aloud, "Oh, no! Here she goes!"

Sugar breaks out in a huge smile, bounces on her toes, and looks excitedly at the boys. They stare at her eagerly waiting for her to solve their problem. She begins "Well, if it was me, I'd act surprised and say, 'Koko? I thought he stayed home with you!'"

Tea buries her face in her hands and whispers to Kandi, "She didn't say that out loud, did she?" Kandi nods and looks away trying not to laugh.

Sugar looks up in the air, closes her eyes, and says, "Or, you could get a little more creative and say he was sucked up by that new robovac that's rolling all over the house and he hasn't figured out how to get out of it yet."

She opens her eyes, claps her hands, and squeals, "Oh, I got it! Just go for the big one and say he was abducted by aliens and taken up on their spaceship!"

Sugar snaps her fingers and says, "Oh, I got a truly believable one. You can just say he went to the kitchen to find something to eat and he'll be back when he's full. Everybody knows that growing boys never get full."

Bouncing on her tiptoes, Sugar whispers, "It might actually go better for you if all of you go missing. That way nobody goes home and nobody gets in trouble. Yes! That's what I'd do if I were you. I wouldn't go home again, ever!"

"Come on, Sugar! You're not helping!" pleads Tea. Kookie looks at Sugar and laughs, "Grandpa Jack may be old, but he's not crazy."

Tea turns to the boys and says, "Ignore what Sugar said—but, what are you going to tell Grandpa Jack?"

Preacher replies, "We're going to tell him the truth!"

Sugar adds, "In that case, you don't have to tell him everything. Leave out all the stuff about Too Cool and the party. Just tell him Koko wasn't ready to come home and he'll be back later. That's true!"

Grace looks at Sugar and shakes her head. "They're already in trouble. Not telling the truth will only make things worse."

Sugar flings her arms in the air and complains, "I'm only trying to help them!" She turns to the boys and says, "I hope to see you later! That is if Grandpa Jack doesn't ground you for the rest of your lives! I'm glad we live on the other side of the water heater. You guys are in so much trouble!"

"SUGAR, PLEASE STOP!" screams Tea.

Kookie bounces her ball and tries to act like everything is okay. She tells the boys, "Don't worry, it will all work out. We'd better head home ourselves. See ya' later!"

"Later!" the boys whisper.

The girls and the boys part ways. As the boys creep home, their antennas drop lower and lower.

Chapter 19
I'm Back!

Triple Point asks his cousins, "What do you think Grandpa Jack is going to say when we tell him what happened?"

Stringbean replies, "I don't know. I'm sure he's going to be upset. He'll probably ground us forever like Sugar said."

Lucky adds, "Well, not going home sounds like a good idea."

Preacher replies, "I'm going home! You guys can do whatever you want to do. I don't want any more trouble."

Suddenly, they hear a voice calling out behind them. When they turn around, they see Koko running excitedly towards them.

"Hey, guys! Wait up! It's me!" screams Koko.

"It's Koko!" shouts Triple Point. Preacher, Lucky, Stringbean, and Triple Point leap happily. Their antennas perk up as they run to greet him.

Overjoyed, Stringbean hugs Koko as tightly as he can. "You're back!" he exclaims. Triple Point looks confused and asks Koko, "What made you leave your 'new' cousins?"

Koko lowers his head and softly says, "I realized I didn't belong there. I'm sorry I talked you into going to that party in the first place. Will you forgive me?"

Preacher laughs, "Of course, we forgive you. We're just glad you're back." Lucky adds, "We're all good now!"

Koko sighs, "Let's go home." Off the boys run home.

Chapter 20
My Bad!

Grandpa Jack is reading the newsfeed on his jTab when the boys arrive. He looks at his watch and says, "The girls just left a short while ago. It doesn't seem like you've had enough time to cook and eat dinner with them. So, where have you been?"

Koko's cousins look at him. Koko replies, "Well... mmm... we kinda met some new friends when we left the gym and decided to play with them for a while."

Grandpa Jack rubs his nose and says, "Hmmp, judging from the way you smell, I'd hope you'd have better taste in friends. You boys smell like burnt rubber!"

Preacher rushes to explain, "It was like this, Koko wanted to be cool and go with Too Cool and his friends. We followed him to a party. We left him there and he caught up with us. Now, we're all home safely. We're sorry and we promise we'll never do it again!"

Lucky quickly adds, "We told Koko we didn't want to go, but we followed him because you told us to always stay together. The closet... it smelled awful. We left, but Koko wanted to stay... so he did."

"And the music... it was so loud... I couldn't hear anything. It made my ears hurt. Koko stayed, but then he left and caught up with us. Now, we're all home," utters Stringbean.

Triple Point looks at Lucky, Stringbean, and Preacher in total disbelief. He declares, "Man! Speaking of motor mouths. You guys can't hold water! Remind me not to do anything around any of you."

Grandpa Jack looks at Koko. He asks him, "So you went to a party with Too Cool and his friends? Weren't you supposed to go help the girls make dinner?

"Yes, sir," replies Koko as he lowers his head and his antennas droop. "I made a mistake. I promise it won't happen again."

Grandpa Jack looks over his spectacles at Koko and says, "It sounds like you made more than a mistake. You made a choice and not a good one."

"What do you mean?" asks Koko. Grandpa Jack, upset with the boys, says "Sit down!" The boys sit on the floor in front of Grandpa Jack.

Grandpa Jack tells them, "There's a big difference between a mistake and a bad choice. We make mistakes when we make choices and don't **know** about the bad results that follow that choice. The first time you make a choice that has a bad result and you don't know about the bad result before you make that choice, it's a mistake and you learn to never make that choice again. The second time you make the exact same choice, it's not a mistake—it's a bad choice you intentionally made because you knew what would happen. Also, when you do something you **know** you're not supposed to do, it's never a mistake—it's a bad choice you made knowing you were not supposed to do it in the first place!"

Grandpa Jack sees the blank expressions on their faces.

"Looks like it's time to bring out another candy bowl experiment!" states Grandpa Jack.

"No, please! No more candy bowls!" begs Koko.

Grandpa Jack chuckles, "No sour balls this time." He goes to the table and picks up two identical candy bowls filled with white cubes. He carries the bowls over to the boys.

Triple Point looks at Koko and blurts, "You know this is all your fault!"

He turns to Grandpa Jack and asks, "Since Koko was the one to make the bad choice, shouldn't he be the one to do the experiment?"

"This is a lesson each of you needs to learn," explains Grandpa Jack. "One of these bowls is filled with sugar cubes and the other bowl is filled with salt cubes,"

Grandpa Jack extends the bowls to Koko and says, "Take a sugar cube and eat it."

Koko looks at the two bowls and then looks at Grandpa Jack. "They both look the same. How am I supposed to know which one has the sugar cubes?" he asks.

"Choose one," replies Grandpa Jack. Koko looks back and forth between the two bowls. He finally takes a cube from one of the bowls and puts it in his mouth. He immediately spits it out.

Koko coughs, "Ewww!!! That's not sugar, it's salt!"

Grandpa Jack explains, "You chose a cube of salt thinking you were choosing a cube of sugar. You didn't know it was salt. That choice was a mistake."

Koko rushes to the table, gets a glass of water, drinks it, and returns to his place on the floor.

Grandpa Jack looks at Koko and sternly says, "You chose to go to a party with Too Cool, even though you **knew** you didn't have my permission. You were even reminded by your cousins that I didn't give you permission to go anywhere but to see the girls, yet you did what you wanted to do. **Was that *a mistake* or *a bad choice?*"**

Koko looks regretfully at Grandpa Jack and replies, "It wasn't a mistake. It was a bad choice. I get it now."

Grandpa Jack replies, "It's okay, Koko! You made the right choice to leave the party and catch up with your cousins."

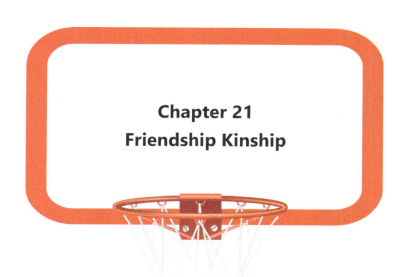

Chapter 21
Friendship Kinship

Grandpa Jack turns his attention to all the boys and says, "Now, let's talk about choosing friends wisely. You can't be friends with everyone you meet. Let's go back to the most important rule for our family—**The Golden Rule: Treat others the way you would want them to treat you!**"

"Koko, how do you want to be treated?" asks Grandpa Jack. Koko thoughtfully answers, "I want to be treated with kindness."

Grandpa Jack comments, "So, kindness is important to you." Koko nods.

"I'm going to ask you the same question, Lucky," states Grandpa Jack. Lucky replies, "I want to be treated fairly."

Grandpa Jack responds, "Okay, so fairness is important to you." Lucky replies, "Yes, sir!"

"Stringbean?" asks Grandpa Jack. Stringbean pauses for a moment and replies, "I want to be told the truth."

Grandpa Jack says, "Hmmm, so truthfulness is important to you."

"Triple Point?" inquires Grandpa Jack. Triple Point replies, "I want others to keep the promises they make to me."

Grandpa Jack says, "So, you want them to be trustworthy." Triple Point answers, "Well,... yes, sir!"

"Preacher?" asks Grandpa Jack. Preacher shrugs and replies, "I want to be listened to and not cut off or made to feel that what I say is not important."

Grandpa Jack looks understandingly at Preacher and says, "In other words, you want to be respected." Preacher looks at Grandpa Jack and replies, "Yes, sir."

Grandpa Jack says, "From what you boys have told me—kindness, fairness, truthfulness, trustworthiness, and respect are important to you." He lifts up the sugar cube bowl in one of his hands. "They're the VALUES you want others to show towards you. Your values are like these sugar cubes when you're expecting sugar."

Grandpa Jack lowers the sugar cube bowl and lifts the bowl of salt cubes. "If someone is mean, unfair, doesn't tell the truth, doesn't keep their word, or disrespects you—their values are like these salt cubes when you are expecting sugar," continues Grandpa Jack.

Koko gives Grandpa Jack a puzzled look and asks, "But when you meet someone you don't know, how can you tell if they're values are sweet or salty?"

"When choosing friends, look at how they behave. Are they kind, respectful, trustworthy, fair, and truthful? Are they polite to everyone, not just to their friends?" replies Grandpa Jack, "If you choose friends who do not have the same values you have, they'll make it hard for you to make good choices."

Stringbean whispers, "You can say that again!"

Grandpa Jack continues, "Friends will never pressure you to do something wrong **and** they aren't afraid to tell you when you are wrong!"

Preacher turns to Koko and explains, "Just like we tried to tell you it was not a good idea to go to that party with Too Cool."

Koko counters, "We're not friends, we're cousins."

"Can't cousins be friends, too?" asks Lucky.

Cousins and Friends!

"Of course, they can! I think we've talked enough about choosing good friends for today," says Grandpa Jack.

Koko jumps to his feet and asks, "Can we go practice with the girls now?"

"Not quite yet," replies Grandpa Jack. "You boys learned some valuable lessons from your misadventure, but there are a few more seeds of wisdom I need to plant. Sit back down."

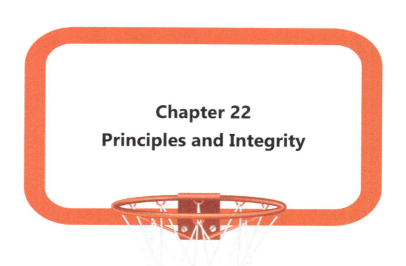

Chapter 22
Principles and Integrity

"Let's discuss integrity," says Grandpa Jack. "Integrity is about doing the right thing, even when you think no one else is looking. We just talked about values, so you know what they are. Now, we need to discuss principles. Integrity is how well you stick to your principles no matter where you are or what others say."

"I don't quite understand!" exclaims Preacher. Grandpa Jack ponders for a second and asks, "You boys know about the rules you follow when you play basketball, right?"

Lucky eagerly responds, "Yes! You can't walk with the ball. You've got to shoot or pass. And, you can't run into another player while you're shooting the ball!"

INTEGRITY is what you do, even when you think no one is looking!

~Unknown Author

Grandpa Jack replies, "Good examples, Lucky. Just like basketball has rules about what you can and can't do on the court, you must have rules about what you will and will not do that guide the choices you make off the court. Those rules are called principles."

"Where do principles come from?" asks Triple Point. Grandpa Jack responds, "The simplest way to answer that question is to say principles are the rules you choose to live by based on your values."

"I don't get it," says Stringbean.

"Okay, let's take for example, I value truthfulness, so 'I will always tell the truth!' is a principle I choose to live by. I value honesty, so 'I will always be honest!' is a principle I live by. I value being on time, so 'I will always be on time!' is a principle I live by. There are plenty of rules I choose to live by. They're my principles," declares Grandpa Jack.

"Oh, I understand now," says Koko.

Grandpa Jack replies, "Good! Always remember our family's moral compass guide: 'Do what's right! If you start right, and stay right, you'll end right!'" He looks at his watch and says, "I think we've discussed enough today. We'll talk more when we call a family meeting with your aunt and the girls."

"Hey, we still have to make up the practice time we didn't put in today. Let's go!" cheers Koko.

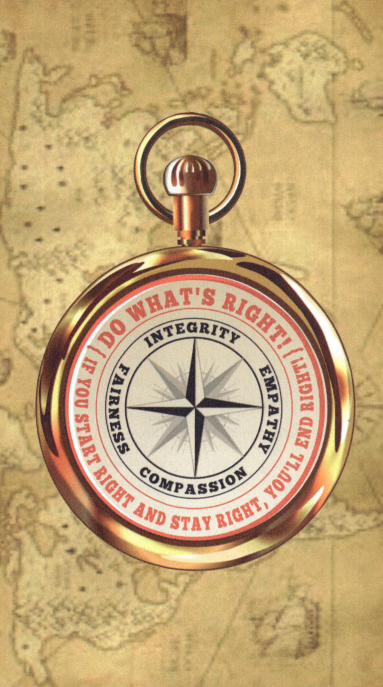

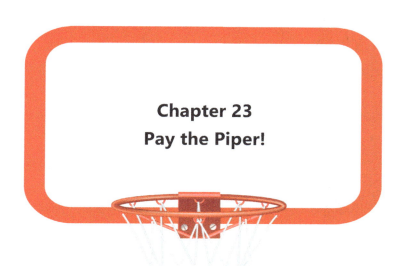

Chapter 23
Pay the Piper!

As the boys jump to their feet and head towards the door, Grandpa Jack lifts up one of his hands and says, "Hold on a minute! You boys danced to the music, now it's time to pay the piper." The boys look at Grandpa Jack as if he's speaking another language.

"Pay the piper?" asks Koko. "What does that mean?"

Triple Point adds, "I don't know what Koko did after we left, but we didn't dance to any music or do anything else." Lucky, Stringbean, and Preacher nod in agreement.

Grandpa Jack chuckles softly and says, "It's an old saying that means, it's time for you to pay the price for the decisions you made."

He continues, "You boys have to understand there are consequences for your actions. Every choice you make—good or bad—has a consequence that you can't get around. Now, you have to deal with the consequences of going to a party without my permission."

"But, it was all my fault. Please don't punish them for what I did," admits Koko. "You told us to always stay together and we'd be safe. They followed me trying to make sure I was safe."

"I understand why they went to the party," replies Grandpa Jack to Koko. "I also understand why you went and why you left. We'll deal with that later."

Grandpa Jack looks at Preacher, Lucky, Stringbean, and Triple Point. He tells them, "In the future, don't do anything that you know is wrong or that doesn't feel right to you. It doesn't matter what Koko or anybody else says or chooses to do: THINK FOR YOURSELF! You don't have to go looking for trouble, it will find you. Trouble is always easy to get into, but may be difficult to get out of. You have to learn to see trouble and walk pass it. Have I made myself clear?"

"Yes, sir," they reply.

Grandpa Jack turns his attention back to Koko. "Ok, give me twenty laps around the gym and fifty push-ups." Koko sighs a breath of relief and replies, "Yes, sir!" He turns and prepares to leave for the gym.

"The rest of you can take a break with the girls until Koko is done with his punishment," adds Grandpa Jack. Preacher tells Grandpa Jack, "We'll do whatever punishment he has to do!"

Koko looks at his cousins and asks. "Why would you choose to run laps and do push-ups with me? You can go and hang out with the girls. I'll be okay." Triple Point puts his arm around Koko's shoulder and says, "That's what real friends do!"

Grandpa Jack smiles to himself as the boys leave for the gym.

THE END

INTEGRITY
is
EVERYTHING!

~Wise Saying

NOTE TO PARENTS

This is just the beginning of the Koko and Friends adventures. Koko and his cousins continue to face real-life challenges, such as bullying and cyberbullying, that they only overcome with a clear set of values and principles in their steadfast determination to become All-Star basketball players. Through hard work and perseverance, they master the fundamentals of basketball, learn how to act and react appropriately to negative peer pressure in peer group settings, and set limits and establish boundaries when they have to interact with Too Cool and his crew. The *Long Shots* eventually play teams from other rooms in the house. Win or lose, they learn the importance of determination, perseverance, winning with humility, and losing with dignity.

Koko and his cousins learn increasingly more about self-discipline, good sportsmanship, and that everyone deserves respect no matter who they are, where they live, how they dress, or what they own. Situations arise that are gender-specific (such as girl empowerment, manning up or standing down, social media and body image, and gender bias). They also interact with bugs with autism spectrum disorder and have physical disabilities.

Although Koko and his cousins get into mischief, they receive guidance and correction from Grandpa Jack and Coach Lovelady. Ultimately, Koko and his cousins develop strong moral compasses as they mature into value-driven, principle-based decision makers.